Delicious English
CARAMEL TREE
www.carameltree.com

Mr. Beethoven and Me

CARAMEL TREE

Chapter 1

Mrs. G and the STRAWBERRY Secret

I've been a volunteer at the Riverside Retirement Residence for four years – since I was seven years old. My friend, Matthew, volunteers here too. Some of the people who live at the RRR are a little scary-looking. Sometimes, they have so many wrinkles it's hard to see their eyes. And some of them don't have any teeth.

Mrs. Gucciardi is different. Mrs. G has brown eyes that sparkle, and she always has a smile on her face. She has lots of big, white teeth, only she keeps them in a jar at night. And she talks with her hands because she's Italian. Like me. She used to be a famous opera singer. Not like me.

Anyway, I was reading to Mrs. G in her room today, but she fell asleep about ten minutes after I started reading. So I'm pretend-practicing the piano by tapping out the notes on her bedside table while I'm waiting for her to wake up again. I'm getting ready for the Beethoven Bonanza competition in two weeks. It's hard to concentrate since she's snoring, but I close my eyes and pretend I'm playing the piano on her bedside table.

"Not so much pedal, dear."

My eyes pop open. "What?"

"Not so much pedal," Mrs. G repeats. She looks down at my sneakers.

I laugh. "Oh. I didn't realize I was using the pedal," I say.

"Was it *Moonlight Sonata*?" she asks.

My mouth drops open. "How did you know?"

"The beat," she says. "If you say the word, STRAWBERRY – it's the same beat. ONE, two, three; TWO, two, three; THREE, two, three; FOUR, two, three... and so on."

I play the notes on my knee and say the word STRAWBERRY at the same time. I grin at Mrs. G. "You're right. Saying STRAWBERRY makes it so much easier."

"Mr. Beethoven himself told me that little secret," Mrs. G says.

"Ludwig van Beethoven?" I say. "The deaf one?" I knew Mrs. G was old, but I didn't know she was *that* old!

Mrs. G nods.

"We were friends, a long time ago," Mrs. G says. "In fact, Ludwig wrote *Moonlight Sonata* for my sister. My baby sister, Giulietta. Gee Gee."

"The one with the blue hair?" I say.

She nods again. "The one that loves purple. Clothes, furniture, food..."

"So, why did Mr. Beethoven write *Moonlight Sonata* for Gee Gee?" I ask.

"That's a bit of a long story, Antonia," Mrs. G says. Then she sits up, and I move her pillows so she's more comfortable.

Then I get comfortable in my chair, too. "I have lots of time," I say.

Chapter 2

Mrs. Gucciardi's Story

"A long time ago, I lived in Vienna, Austria," Mrs. G says. "Gee Gee and I both took piano lessons, but she practiced more than me. I preferred singing."

"Because you were training to be a famous opera singer, right?" I ask.

She nods. "Anyway, one evening Gee Gee was practicing a Beethoven song. I heard her crying a couple of times because she couldn't get the song to sound right."

"I don't cry, but it is frustrating when it doesn't sound right," I agree.

"Yes, it is. So then Gee Gee said to me, 'I wish a real musician would come and play this song for me so I could hear how it should sound.' Well, all at once we heard a knock on the door."

"Was it a musician?" I ask.

Mrs. G nods. "None other than Mr. Beethoven. Ludwig. We recognized him at once because of his wavy hair and his frown. He asked to come in.

My parents weren't home, but we opened the door, introduced ourselves, and invited him into the living room. He went to the piano at once. He smiled when he saw the music Gee Gee had been playing. 'This is one of my favorite songs,' he said. Then he looked at my sister. 'May I?' he asked." Mrs. G waves her arm as if she is making the request.

"Gee Gee nodded and pulled the piano bench out for him. I sat down on the sofa, but Gee Gee stayed beside Mr. Beethoven. I thought her face would crack. She was smiling so big."

"Wow!" I say. "I can't believe you actually heard Beethoven play his own song. And on your own piano!"

"Yes, Antonia, but that's not all that happened. As Mr. Beethoven played, the full moon came up. It shone right into our living room and filled the room with soft, yellow moonlight. As he played, Mr. Beethoven watched my sister."

"He could play without looking at his fingers?" I ask.

Mrs. G nods. "And my sister was very beautiful. Lots of men stared at her. When Mr. Beethoven finished, he stood up and bowed to us. 'The secret is in your fingers – keep them curved, like a waterfall,' he said. He told us the STRAWBERRY secret. Then without even saying goodnight, he left."

"That's amazing!" I say. "Did you ever see him again?"

Mrs. G shakes her head. "But he had left us a gift on the piano. And a few days later, we found several sheets of music which had been slipped under the door. And do you know what song he had written on those sheets of music?"

I shake my head.

Mrs. G grins. "*Moonlight Sonata* – the very song you're learning to play now, Antonia. And that's not all – Mr. Beethoven had signed the last sheet of the music. He wrote: *To Giulietta – Thank you for being such a beautiful moonlight inspiration. Remember the waterfall fingers. Sincerely, Ludwig van Beethoven.*"

"Do you mean that *Moonlight Sonata* was written for Gee Gee? Your sister with the blue hair?" I ask.

Mrs. G nods. "Yes, indeed."

Chapter 3

Mr. Beethoven's Bust

"Wow," I say. "I wish I could meet Mr. Beethoven. Then he could help me get ready for the Beethoven Bonanza. It's coming up in a few weeks, and Hannah Mae almost always wins. That's why I'm learning to play *Moonlight Sonata*, so I can win. I think it's Beethoven's best song."

Mrs. G nods, then opens the drawer of her night table.

"Your treasure sack!" I say. "Is Mr. Beethoven in there?"

Mrs. G laughs, "Not exactly." Then she pulls out a small white statue. It's the head and shoulders of a frowning man with wavy hair.

"This is called a bust – Beethoven's bust," Mrs. G says. "He gave it to Gee Gee, well, Gee Gee and me, and I think it might help you."

I look at the bust. "It's nice, but how could it help me?"

"Well," Mrs. G says. "The instructions that came with the bust are a little complicated. But they worked for Gee Gee. She was a concert pianist before she retired. You're very good at talking with your hands, Antonia. Do you think you could act like a symphony conductor?"

I wave my arms around. "Like this?"

She nods. "Well, take this bust home and put it on top of your piano. Then pretend you're conducting a large symphony with about 175 musicians. If you do that, I think you'll get the help you need."

"Should I do it when I'm practicing the piano?" I ask.

"Yes, before you start practicing. But you must be alone in the room. Close the door. In fact, you should put a 'Keep Out' sign on the door. And keep the bust in a safe hiding place."

"I don't know what my mother will think," I say. "But I'll give it a try."

That night, I go into the living room after dinner. "I have to practice the piano," I tell my mom. "Please don't let anybody in the living room. Especially Fabio."

She's busy trying to buy some shoes online. Without even looking at me, she says, "Alright, dear."

I close the living room door. Then I get the bust out of my backpack and set it on the piano. Mr. Beethoven looks very serious. In fact, his eyebrows make him look angry. I play my scales for a few minutes so Mom won't get suspicious. Then I stand up and look around to make sure Fabio isn't hiding in the room.

I pick up a pencil and start conducting. I close my eyes and try to imagine 175 instruments: violins and violas; trombones and trumpets. 175 musicians all staring at me, and I'm the boss! I can hear *Moonlight Sonata* inside my head.

"All right, all right. Are you trying to fly?" a gruff voice says.

My eyes pop open. My mouth drops open.

Chapter 4

My First Lesson with Mr. Beethoven

He's standing in the middle of my living room. Ludwig van Beethoven! I know it's him right away because of the bust, and I've seen his picture in my piano book. He's dressed in an old-fashioned velvet suit with fancy short pants and a big puffy tie. His hair looks like Mrs. G's. It's gray and wavy and almost touches his shoulders.

"Mr. B... B... B... Beethoven," I stammer.

"Indeed," he says. "Ludwig van Beethoven. Now, what can I do for you – Antonia, is it?"

"How do you know my name?" I yell.

His eyebrows relax and he smiles. "My old friend, Mrs. Gucciardi, told me about you," he says. "She told me you're a very good pianist."

"Oh," I say. "Well, I'm trying to learn one of your songs. *Moonlight Sonata*. It's my favorite."

"Ah, yes. The song I composed for lovely Giulietta," he says. He points to the piano bench. "May I?"

"Yes, please, Mr. Beethoven," I say.

He sits down and plays the first few bars. Then he stands up, and I play the same thing. "No, no, no," he says. "Relax. Play with your heart. Not your mind. Think of the soft yellow moonlight on a summer night. Pretend you are asleep and dreaming about something you love."

We move on to the next line. "Not so much pedal," he says. "Waterfall fingers, not claws. The music must flow from your fingertips."

"But you're a brilliant composer," I say. "I'm just an ordinary girl."

He shakes his head. "A girl, yes. Ordinary, no. You can be a brilliant musician, too." He puts one hand on my shoulder. "May I tell you a secret, Antonia? A one-word secret?"

I nod my head. He bends down closer to me. "Practice. You must practice. When I was your age, I practiced 8, 10, even 12 hours a day."

Before I can say anything, somebody knocks on the door. "Are you all right in there, Antonia?" Mom asks. "Who are you talking to?"

"Um... just myself," I say. "I'm fine, Mom." I wait for a few seconds, but she doesn't respond. She is probably busy chasing Fabio around. Back to the piano.

After two hours, my fingers and my brain are too tired to play anymore. Before he disappears, Mr. Beethoven says, "Remember, you must practice at least two hours a day, Antonia. Just wave your arms like a conductor, and I'll come to help you."

I nod. "Yes, Mr. Beethoven. Thank you, sir." Then I put the bust in my backpack, and he disappears.

The next day, I go to the RRR to thank Mrs. G for my special tutor. I tell her all about my lesson with Mr. Beethoven last night. When I finish my story, she gives me a big smile. "Keep it secret, won't you?" she says. I nod.

"One more thing, Antonia," Mrs. G says. "You will only be able to call on him ten times. After that, you must pass the bust on to someone else. So, be sure to call on him *only* when you need him."

I nod again. I'm sure ten lessons with Mr. B himself will be more than enough to help me win the Beethoven Bonanza.

Chapter 5

Wasted Lessons

Every day for the rest of the week, I practice for two hours a day. My arms ache, both from playing the piano and from pretending I'm conducting a symphony. But Mr. Beethoven comes to help me every day.

I keep track of the number of times he has appeared. After four lessons, I don't think I'm much better at all. Still, I have six more lessons and another week before the Bonanza.

On Friday, I have a soccer game after dinner. I get up early in the morning to practice the piano before school. Mom, Dad, and Fabio are all very grumpy at breakfast time. "Why do you make so much noise so early, Antonia?" Fabio says.

"I have to practice," I say. "The Beethoven Bonanza is in seven days."

I'm not a very good soccer player. Nobody ever passes me the ball. I stand close to the net, wave my arms in the air and yell at Hannah Mae. "I'm open!" I yell. "Pass!"

Suddenly, I see him. Mr. Beethoven. I look at my backpack. The bust has fallen out and is lying on the ground. Mr. B is sitting in the stands with all the other parents who are wearing shorts and T-shirts. He is wearing his velvet suit, as always.

"Hello, Antonia!" he yells. Does this count as one of the ten times I can call on him to help me? I look around, but there is no piano on the soccer field – it's a wasted opportunity.

Just then, Hannah Mae passes me the ball. But I'm looking at Mr. Beethoven, so the ball hits me in the cheek. The other team steals the ball and scores a goal. For the rest of the game, I make sure I keep my arms down by my sides. It's very hard to run without moving your arms.

After the game, Mom says, "Who was that strange man yelling at you? He seemed to be a little overdressed for a soccer game."

"Um... he was just somebody from the RRR," I say. "Mr. B. He's a friend of Mrs. G's."

"Maybe she could help him pick out some new clothes," she says.

I nod.

On Saturday morning, I get up early. I have cheerleading practice after lunch. I put the bust on the piano, close my eyes and start conducting.

"Did you score a goal yesterday?"

My eyes pop open. "No, Mr. Beethoven. I play soccer almost as badly as I play the piano."

"Practice makes perfect," he says. "Shall we?"

We take turns playing each section. "More contrast," he says. "The crescendos must really stand out in this song. Think of them as brilliant, sparkling moonbeams on a cold winter night."

By the end of two hours, I am very tired of *Moonlight Sonata.* I am also very tired of the word, STRAWBERRY. I can't erase it from my brain. I don't think I will ever eat another strawberry, even though it's my favorite fruit, next to blueberries. But the Beethoven Bonanza is only six days away. I must keep practicing.

After lunch, Mom drives me to cheerleading practice. I'm the smallest girl on the cheerleading team, so I'm always on top of the pyramids. Hannah Mae is always underneath me. "Who was that weird looking guy at the soccer game yesterday?" she asks.

I shrug. "Just somebody from the retirement home."

"So, what song are you playing for the Beethoven Bonanza this year?" she asks.

"I haven't decided yet."

She stares up at me. "Are you kidding? It's next Friday!"

I shrug again.

When it comes time to practice our finale, I get in the middle of the line. We all wave our pom poms around in the air like windmills. After I do my final flip, I see Mr. Beethoven waving to me from the sidelines. The bust has fallen out of my backpack again. I really must remember to take time to zip it up properly. Now, I've wasted another lesson.

"Why does that old man keep following you around?" Hannah Mae asks. "And why does he dress like that?"

"He's lonely, I guess," I say. "And old-fashioned."

Chapter 6

I Can't Use My Hands!

On Monday morning, Mrs. Dill, our music teacher, takes us to the Concert Hall where the Bonanza will be. She wants us to get comfortable with the place. She asks, "Who can name three of Beethoven's famous symphonies?"

I put my hand up a bit too quickly. Then I see *him* again. Oh no! Another wasted lesson!

The kids all start whispering and laughing. I put my hand down and check my backpack. It's closed. I guess just moving my arms when I'm wearing my backpack also calls him. When I look up again, he's gone.

"That guy is creepy. Is he a ghost or something?" Hannah Mae asks.

"What guy?" I say. "I didn't see anybody."

She frowns at me.

That night, I decide I must speak with Mr. B about showing up all the time.

"Mr. Beethoven," I say after the practice is finished. "I wonder... could you please only come when I'm practicing the piano?"

He looks a little embarrassed. "Oh, I'm sorry. It's just that whenever you wave your arms in the air, I think it's because you need me."

I try to explain that waving my hands when I talk or play soccer is not the same as waving my hands when I conduct an orchestra. But he says he can't tell the difference. "You'll just need to stop waving your hands around so much," he says.

"Stop waving my hands?" I say. "That's impossible!" I look up, but I'm talking to empty air.

The next day in the cafeteria, I see Hannah Mae and Jody. They're sitting in the corner. I pretend I don't see them waving at me while I am waiting in line for my pizza and carrot sticks. I don't want to wave back and waste my last lesson with Mr. Beethoven.

"Antonia," Hannah Mae yells. "Why are you ignoring me?"

My face turns red. I quickly pick up a tray with both hands so I don't have to wave. I turn around to smile at Hannah Mae, but she and Jody are giggling.

"She walks like a robot," I hear one of them say.

It sure is hard not to move my arms when I speak. Anyway, I only have one more lesson, and then I'll be free to move my arms as much as I want.

After supper, I put Beethoven's bust on the piano, close the door, and start conducting. This is my last chance to get help from the great man himself. If only I hadn't wasted so many lessons.

"Good evening, Antonia," he says. "Have you been practicing?"

I hold up my sore fingers. My fingertips almost have calluses on them from playing the piano for hours and hours every day. "I think I've almost got it perfect," I say. Then I sit down and play *Moonlight Sonata*. He doesn't interrupt me, or correct me, not even once. And I don't even have to look at my fingers or the music.

When I'm finished, I release the pedal and look up at him. He's resting his cheek on one hand and leaning his elbow on top of the piano. Is he crying? He wipes his eyes, and then smiles.

"Beautiful, Antonia. Simply beautiful. I couldn't have played it better myself," he says. "And just as well, because today is your final lesson. I don't think you need me anymore. In my head, I could hear the entire orchestra playing behind you."

I grin. "Really?"

I hug him. He smells like my grandmother's attic.

Just then, Fabio bangs on the door. "Are you done, Antonia? I want a turn playing the piano now."

I pick up Mr. Beethoven's bust from the piano. The funny thing is, he's not frowning anymore. He's smiling! I look up at the real Mr. Beethoven before I put the

bust in my backpack. But he's gone, and I'm looking at empty air. But I can still hear him, whispering. "Goodbye, Antonia. And good luck. You will perform beautifully, I'm sure of it. And hang on to my bust. Maybe one day your little brother will need my assistance."

I wipe my eyes and open the door. Fabio and I sit down together on the piano bench. "No, Fabio. Not claws. Make your fingers like a waterfall. Let the music flow."

He looks at me like I've got two heads. But he tries to do what I tell him.

Chapter 7

The Beethoven Bonanza

On Friday night, we stop by the RRR to pick up Mrs. G. I've been so busy practicing that I haven't had time to visit her for two weeks.

"How did you get along with Ludwig?" she whispers.

I smile at her. "He's awesome," I say. "I wish he could be here tonight."

We arrive at the Concert Hall early. Mr. Beethoven's bust is in my backpack, right next to my music for *Moonlight Sonata*.

"Are you nervous?" Hannah Mae asks me.

I shake my head. "Not really. I've been practicing a lot."

"I had five extra piano lessons this week," she says. "It was really expensive, but my piano teacher is a Beethoven expert. He knows everything about Beethoven and his music."

"Really?" I say. I put my hand inside my backpack and find Mr. Beethoven's bust. It feels like he's smiling so big his face might crack.

When it's finally my turn, it's already dark outside. My stomach feels a little nervous, but I remember Mr. Beethoven's instructions. '*Relax. Play with your heart. Not your mind.*' I adjust the bench so it's the right height for me. Then I sit down and spread out my music, even though I have the whole song memorized. I make my fingers into a waterfall, then I look down at my hands. They're glowing! I look up at the stained glass window. Brilliant beams of moonlight are lighting up my hands. And I'm pretty sure I can hear Mr. Beethoven's voice. "Beautiful, Antonia," he's saying. "Simply beautiful."

I close my eyes, put my foot on the pedal, relax, and play with my heart, not my mind. By the end, I can hear all the instruments, all 175 of them. Before I know it, I'm finished. I blink several times, then I stand up and take a bow. The applause is really loud. I open my eyes

and look out at the audience. I wave to Mom and Dad, Fabio, and Mrs. G. They're standing up and clapping, which is really embarrassing. I wave some more and look all around the hall, but he's not there. I smile.

When I go back to my seat, Mrs. G squeezes my hand. "Ludwig would be so proud of you, Antonia," she whispers.

"Thanks for letting me use your bust," I say. "Do you want it back?"

Mrs. G holds up her crooked fingers. "My piano playing days are behind me," she says. "You keep the bust, dear. You can pass it on to someone one day."

Hannah Mae plays *Fur Elise*, a little too quickly I think, but I'm not surprised when the judges say they can't choose between us, as we both played our songs almost perfectly. "We have two first-place winners this year," they say. "Congratulations, girls."

And the prize? Well, it's something I already have, only this one looks like it's made of bronze. And he's frowning. I smile and put it in my backpack, right next to my other one.

When I get home, I put the bronze one on top of the piano. And Mrs. G's bust? Well, I find a nice safe hiding place on the top shelf in my closet. I'll keep it for Fabio. He might want to play in the Beethoven Bonanza someday, too. If he does, I'll share the STRAWBERRY secret with him, too.

Then I go downstairs and start practicing a new song...